FROM GRAN WITH LOVE

Created and Written by

Bella Neville Cruz and Mom (Katia Q.Cruz)

Edited by Sarah Fabiny • Illustrated by Madeleine Mae B. Migallos

Tellwell Talent
www.tellwell.ca

ISBN
978-0-2288-5562-0 (Hardcover)
978-0-2288-5561-3 (Paperback)

Dedicated to

mi Abi (mi Abuela, that means my Grandma)

and mi Mamá (my Mom).

Inspired by some of my family situations and events. I thank Mamá and Papá for all their Love and Support.

BELLA♥
★
KGC mom

Bella and her grandmother were sitting on the front porch together. Bella turned to her grandmother and asked, "Will you love me even when I drink all your water?" Grandma turned to Bella and answered, "I might be thirsty, but I will still love you."

Bella: Will you love me when I am reading your book?

Grandma: I am going to be frustrated, but I will still love you. Perhaps you can read it to me!

Bella: Will you love me even when I am hiding from you?

Grandma: I would be confused, but I will still love you. And I would come find you.

Bella: Will you love me when I am using your markers?

Grandma: I will be bored. I won't be able to draw, but I will still love you. And you can draw a picture for me.

Bella: Are you going to love me if I make many pictures for you?

Grandma: Of course! I will be full of art, but I will still love you.

Bella: Will you love me when I jump on the couch?

Grandma: I will be scared. And I might shout! But that is because I love you; I do not want you to fall down.

Bella: If I come to your bed because I want a hug ... will you love me then?

Grandma: I will feel warm, loved, and cared for. I will love you even more.

Grandma hugged Bella, gave her a kiss, and said, "I will always love you no matter how you feel or whatever you do!"

Bella: I will love you forever and ever, Grandma.

About the Author:

Bella is a bright, loving, five-year-old. She is a very happy girl who likes to sing and dance. Bella speaks English and Spanish. She also loves to draw and paint and make up stories. We hope that you enjoy this one.

Katia is Bella's mom. She always puts the needs of family and friends first. She helped arrange the ideas and the words. She is the one who did all the background work to get this story to you.

CPSIA information can be obtained
at www.ICGtesting.com
Printed in the USA
BVHW020639310821
615082BV00002B/66